Jake, the Juggler

Written by Jill Eggleton

Illustrated by Kelvin Hawley

The people in the book

The kitchen in the book

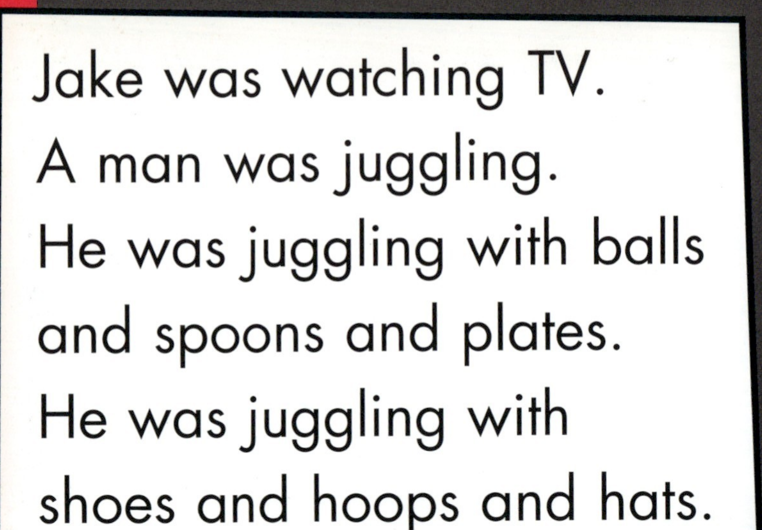

Jake was watching TV.
A man was juggling.
He was juggling with balls
and spoons and plates.
He was juggling with
shoes and hoops and hats.

"I can juggle like that,"
said Jake.

Jake went into the kitchen.
He looked in the cabinet.

Jake saw some bananas.

"I can juggle with bananas," he said.

The bananas went...
UP,
UP,
UP.
"Cool," shouted Jake.
"I'm juggling!"

A banana went on the floor.

A banana went on the chair.

"**OOPS!**" said Jake.
"**Bananas are no good.**
I can't juggle with bananas."

Jake looked in the refrigerator.

Jake saw some tomatoes.

"I can juggle with tomatoes,"
he said.

The tomatoes went...
UP,
UP,
UP.
"Cool," shouted Jake.
"I'm juggling!"

A tomato went on the floor.

A tomato went on the chair.

A tomato went on the cat!

“OOPS!” said Jake.
**“Tomatoes are no good.
I can’t juggle with tomatoes.”**

The cat is...?

Jake got grapes. 

He got peas. 

He got beans. 

Grapes and peas and beans went all over the room.

"They're no good," said Jake. **"They're too small."**

Jake got potatoes.

He got cabbages.

He got pumpkins.

Potatoes, cabbages, and pumpkins went all over the room.

"They're no good," said Jake. "They're too big."

Jake's mom came
into the kitchen!
It was a **big** mess!

"Jake," she said.
"What are you doing?"

"I'm juggling," said Jake.

"Look at this kitchen,"
said his mom.
"It's a big mess!
You will have to clean it up."

Jake will...

clean up?

not clean up?

Jake had to clean up the kitchen.
Then his mom got...
a sock,
some rice,
a needle,
some thread.
And she made Jake some juggling balls!

“Now you can juggle,”
she said.
“But go outside!”

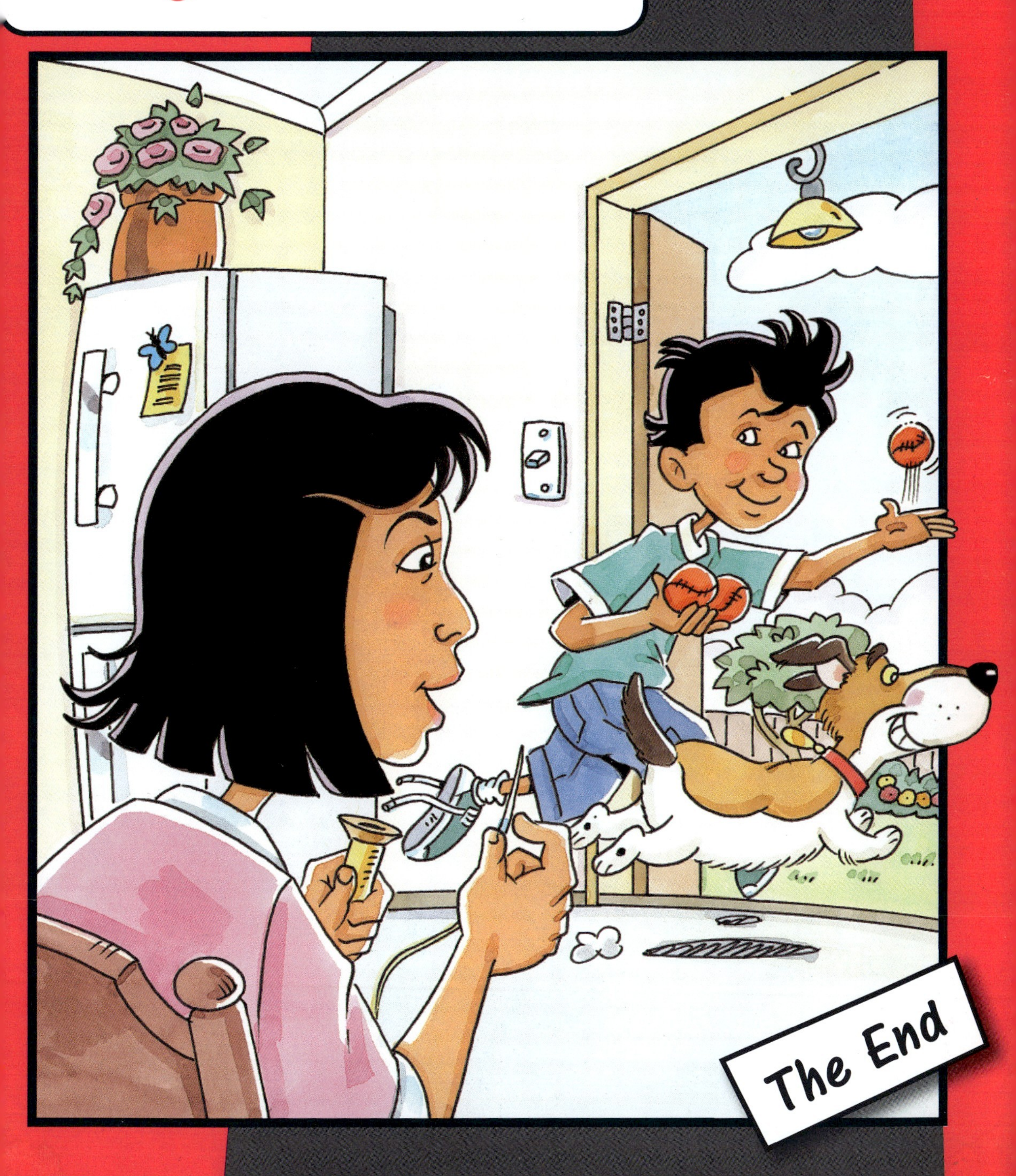

Lists

Things to juggle with:

pillows 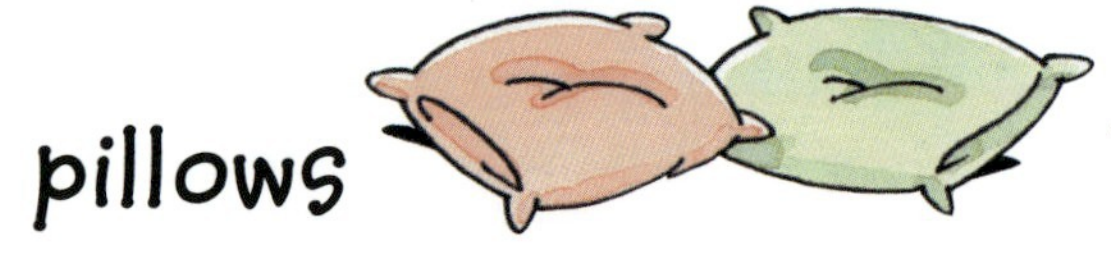 Yes? No?

oranges  Yes? No?

books  Yes? No?

blocks  Yes? No?

pens  Yes? No?

Things to juggle with:

chairs  Yes? No?

balls  Yes? No?

cats  Yes? No?

apples  Yes? No?

potatoes  Yes? No?

Word Bank

balls 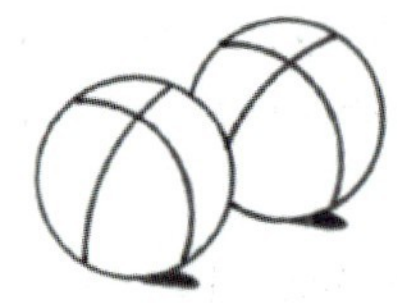

bananas 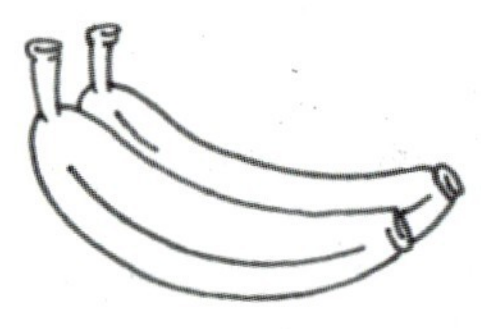

cups 

hats 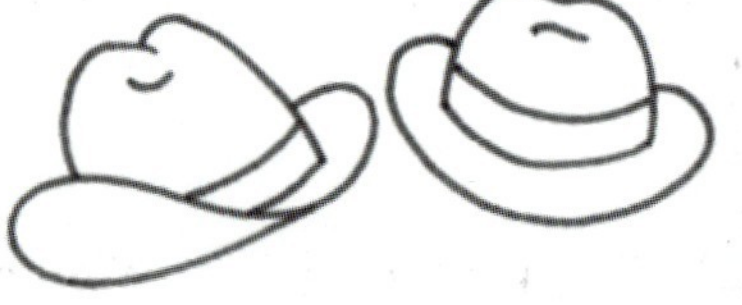

hoops 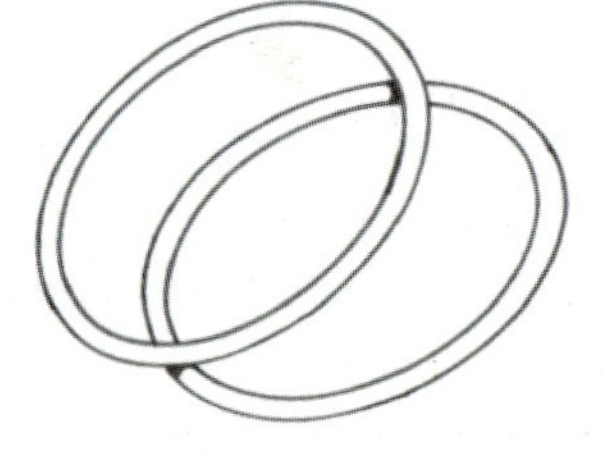

knives 

plates 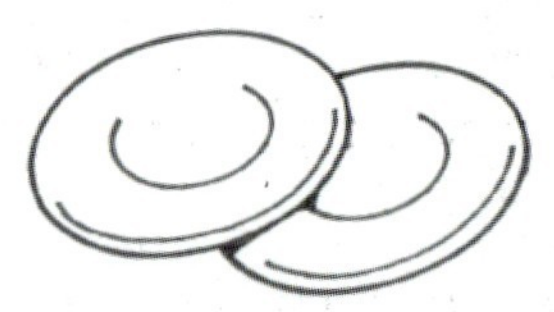

refrigerator 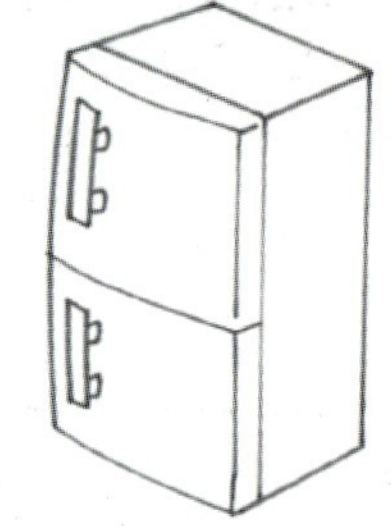

shoes 

spoons 

tomatoes